PUFFIN BOOKS

Viking in Trouble

Jeremy Strong once worked in a bakery, putting the jam into 3,000 doughnuts every night. Now he puts the jam in stories instead, which he finds much more exciting. At the age of three he fell out of a first-floor bedroom window and landed on his head. His mother says that this damaged him for the rest of his life and refuses to take any responsibility. He loves writing stories because he says it is 'the only time you alone have complete control and can make anything happen'. His ambition is to make you laugh (or at least snuffle). Jeremy Strong lives in Kent with his wife, Susan, two cats, and a pheasant that sits on the garden fence with a 'can't catch me' grin on his beak.

Jeremy Strong

Viking in Trouble

Illustrated by John Levers

PUFFIN BOOKS

PUFFIN BOOKS

Published by the Penguin Group
Penguin Books Ltd, 80 Strand, London WC2R 0RL, England
Penguin Putnam Inc., 375 Hudson Street, New York, New York 10014, USA
Penguin Books Australia Ltd, 250 Camberwell Road, Camberwell, Victoria 3124, Australia
Penguin Books Canada Ltd, 10 Alcorn Avenue, Toronto, Ontario, Canada M4V 3B2
Penguin Books India (P) Ltd, 11 Community Centre, Panchsheel Park, New Delhi – 110 017, India
Penguin Books (NZ) Ltd, Cnr Rosedale and Airborne Roads, Albany, Auckland, New Zealand
Penguin Books (South Africa) (Pty) Ltd, 24 Sturdee Avenue, Rosebank 2196, South Africa

Penguin Books Ltd, Registered Offices: 80 Strand, London WC2R 0RL, England

www.penguin.com

First published by A & C Black Ltd 1992
Published in Puffin Books 1995
14

Text copyright © Jeremy Strong, 1992
Illustrations copyright © John Levers, 1992
All rights reserved

The moral right of the author (and illustrator) has been asserted

Made and printed in England by Clays Ltd, St Ives plc

British Library Cataloguing in Publication Data
A CIP catalogue record for this book is available from the British Library

ISBN 0–140–37481–7

This is for 'Berserkers' everywhere

Trouble Ahead

The Viking Hotel in Flotby was famous throughout Britain – not for its fine cooking or excellent sea-views – but because it had a real Viking living and working there. People came from far and wide to see Sigurd. He was, after all, quite a sight. He had a fiercesome black beard and moustache and somehow managed to draw attention to himself wherever he went. This may have had something to do with the way he waved his huge sword 'Nosepicker' about his head.

Nobody was quite sure how Sigurd came to be in Flotby at the end of the twentieth century, but Siggy had a strange story to tell.

'I from Hedeby in Denmark. I sail with Ulric Blacktooth. Sit on boat long time and get dead bottom. Big war fleet. We come to kill everyone and steal everything. But mist come like cloud of darkness, all spooky-wooky. Boats go in mist, can't see, like helmet slip down too far. We listen to sea. I sit at front of ship and ship go bang-bang against rocks. I fall off. Splash. Very wet, very cold. I get up. Where boat? Boat gone. I climb up cliff. I come to house. Agh! It's me! Outside is sign with me – Viking Hotel. I walk in. Here I am. I am Sigurd from Hedeby in Denmark. Good morning and welcome! Hot baths in every room. Very well thank you. The toilets are over there. Goodnight!'

At this point Sigurd would bow to his audience and there would be much applause. He had told this story many times. After all, he had been living at The Viking Hotel for almost a year now. Poor Mr and Mrs Ellis, the owners of the hotel, had been driven quite mad by him.

The problem was very simple. Siggy had come straight out of the tenth century and into the twentieth. A lot of things had changed since 900AD, and Siggy was still trying to get used to them. Meanwhile Mr and Mrs Ellis were still trying to get used to *him*.

The Ellis's children, Tim and Zoe, thought that Siggy was marvellous. They enjoyed showing him off to their friends and Zoe had even undertaken the hard task of trying to teach Sigurd some English.

Then there was Mrs Tibblethwaite, the widower who had first come to the hotel as a guest, but had stayed on – and on – and on. It wasn't much of a secret that Siggy was madly in love with her, or that Tibby, as she was affectionately known, had a very large soft spot for the daft Viking. It seemed quite obvious that they would get married.

The decision bit was simple, but after that it got very complicated and very noisy.

'We have Viking weeding!' announced Sigurd.

'Wedding, not weeding,' corrected Zoe.

'Ah! Viking wedding!' shouted Siggy, waving Nosepicker above his head and slicing through the lampshade. There was a loud bang as the hotel electrics fused and everything went dark.

'Who am I?' bellowed Sigurd, crashing into a near-by table.

'Not "Who am I?". You say "*Where* am I?".'

Mr Ellis heaved a deep sigh and made his way to the fuse box. A few minutes passed and the lights came back on. Siggy was on his feet in an instant, wildly waving his sword. 'Where did that? Sigurd kill him!'

'There's no need to kill anyone Sigurd. And you don't say "Where did that?" You must say "*Who* did that?".'

'Who did that?' Sigurd repeated slowly.

'Who did what?' asked Mr Ellis, coming back into the room.

Siggy looked at Mr Ellis, then at Zoe, and tried to puzzle out the new turn in the conversation. It was too much. His eyes narrowed to dark slits. 'I kill him!' he hissed.

'Kill who?' asked Mr Ellis, completely mystified.

Mrs Tibblethwaite could stand it no longer. She rose majestically to her feet and bellowed at everyone. 'That is quite enough of this gibberish. Perhaps we can get back to making the arrangements for the wedding. We shall have a church wedding, with a vicar and a white dress and a veil.'

Tim giggled and whispered to his sister. 'I didn't think vicars wore white dresses with veils.'

'Sssh! That's not what Tibby means.'

Zoe's reply was almost drowned out by the noise of Sigurd clambering on to a dining table. 'By Odin!' he thundered, 'I say we have a Viking weeding. We kill ten sheep, five cows, eight pigs and forty chickens. We make fire for Thor to bless our weeding. Then you Viking woman.'

Mrs Tibblethwaite hitched up her skirts and climbed up on the table beside her future husband. 'Just a moment, Sigurd. We are not going to sacrifice anything. I shall have a white weeding dress – oh bother you! I mean a white wedding dress, and we will be married in a church by a vicar or we won't be married at all.'

'Viking weeding!' bellowed Sigurd, waving Nosepicker alarmingly close to the light again.

'Church!' screeched Mrs Tibblethwaite, stamping her foot on the table. All of a sudden there was an almighty crash as the table collapsed beneath their weight. Sigurd and Tibby vanished from sight, emerging seconds later as a struggling heap on the ground.

They clung to each other as they struggled back to their feet.

'All right, you win Siggy,' laughed Mrs Tibblethwaite. But the Viking bowed low to her.

'We marry in church,' he said. 'I am yours forever.'

Tim turned away in disgust. 'Yuk!' he muttered. 'I think I'm going to be sick.'

Having finally agreed on the arrangements for the wedding, Sigurd and Mrs Tibblethwaite went to visit the vicar. Everything was going fine until the vicar asked Sigurd what his surname was.

'Surname?' repeated Sigurd, completely bewildered.

'Yes. My surname is Buttertubs. What is yours?'

'Buttertubs?'

'Ah – so your name is Sigurd Buttertubs. That's quite unusual for a Viking, I think.'

Mrs Tibblethwaite butted in. 'Of course his name isn't Buttertubs. He doesn't know what you are talking about. Do you think I'd marry anyone called Sigurd Buttertubs? If he has to have a surname call him 'Viking'. It's as good as anything else.'

And so the marriage of Sigurd and Mrs Tibblethwaite went ahead. Tibby got her wish and arrived in a flowing white wedding gown and veil. Sigurd got his wish too. Halfway through the ceremony he threw a pile of twigs on the church floor, set them on fire and raised both his arms.

'Hear me Thor,' he thundered. 'Bless this wedding. Make Mrs Tibblethwaite happy. Make . . .'

Sigurd's touching speech was brought to an abrupt end as the vicar frantically baled water out of the font and over the fire. There was a loud hiss, followed by clouds of smoke and the guests ran coughing from the church and headed straight for The Viking Hotel to begin the celebrations. Mr Ellis opened several bottles of champagne. Siggy seemed to think that the delicate little glasses were just *too* little to drink out of. He seized a water jug and threw the contents to one side.

There was a startled squeak. 'Eeek! I'm soaked! I'm flooded! My new dress!' cried the vicar's wife, as she stared open-mouthed at her soaking dress.

Sigurd was crestfallen. 'Very sorry, I make you better,' he said and began to brush down Mrs Buttertubs with his huge hairy hands. At once she started screaming again.

'Eeek! Get off me you brute! Don't touch me or I shall call the police! Help – police!'

Mrs Ellis came to her rescue. She guided Sigurd away and went back to help Mrs Buttertubs recover. Meanwhile Sigurd had opened two more bottles of champagne, poured them into the water jug and was sitting in an armchair. He gazed lovingly across the room at his new wife and raised his jug of champagne to her.

'Ears!' he shouted.

'Ears?' muttered Mr Ellis. 'Ears?'

Zoe giggled quietly. 'I think he means "cheers" Dad.' Mr Ellis began to laugh. Soon everyone was going round the room saying 'Ears!' to each other and raising their glasses.

Then some bright spark started saying 'Legs!' instead. The laughter got louder and louder.

The only silent person now was Sigurd, who was completely baffled. Zoe sat down next to him, tears rolling down her cheeks. She tried to explain, but every time she began she was overcome with laughter.

Nobody saw the small thin man in the dark suit enter the room and glance round suspiciously. He spoke seriously to each guest in turn until at last he came to Mr Ellis.

'Excuse me,' he said, in a voice that sounded as if it came from inside a very small tin can. 'But my name is Mr Thripp. I have been staying at your hotel for the last four days.'

'Jolly good,' laughed Mr Ellis. 'Hope you're enjoying yourself.'

Mr Thripp pressed closer. 'Actually, I can't say that I have. You see Mr Ellis, I work for the Health Department. I have been very concerned to see that the meals in this hotel are being served by one of the filthiest, dirtiest, most disgusting waiters I have ever seen in my life.'

By this time Mr Ellis was on red alert. 'Just what do you mean, Mr Thripp?' he demanded.

'I mean that so-called Viking of yours. He is a public health hazard. He is revolting. I am going to have to report this hotel to the Health Department, which means that unless you do something about him straight away, you will be closed down. Good day, Mr Ellis.'

The thin man slipped away through the guests like a slug through leaves. Mr Ellis stood quite still, the colour gone from his face and the enjoyment of the last few hours completely forgotten.

2

Taxi!

When Mr Ellis told everyone about the Health Inspector's visit, they were all understandably upset . . . especially Sigurd . . . 'I not dirty!' he cried, banging both fists on his chest. Clouds of dust erupted from his furry top and several moths decided it was time to leave.

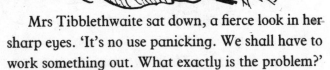

Mrs Tibblethwaite sat down, a fierce look in her sharp eyes. 'It's no use panicking. We shall have to work something out. What exactly is the problem?'

Mr Ellis sighed deeply. 'The problem is that if we don't find Siggy another job the hotel will be closed down and we shall go bankrupt.'

Tibby looked surprisingly cheerful. 'I really don't see what all the fuss is about. The answer is quite clear. We take my dear husband out of the kitchen and give him something else to do.'

'Like what?' asked Zoe.

'Making the beds? Gardening? Cleaning rooms?' suggested Mrs Tibblethwaite.

Mr and Mrs Ellis looked at each other thoughtfully. It hadn't taken long to teach the Viking how to wait at table. Maybe he could be taught how to do something else. Mr Ellis stood up.

'Right then Siggy, how would you like to be a chambermaid?'

'Dad – he can't be a chambermaid! He'll have to be a chamberviking!' giggled Tim. Mr Ellis smiled. Sigurd looked puzzled.

'I want you to clean the bedrooms, Siggy. Understand?'

'I understand. I clean beetroots.'

'Not beetroots – bedrooms. Mr Johnson is leaving Room Nine. I want you to get all the bed linen from his bed and take it to the laundry room, okay?'

'Okey-dokey boss,' Sigurd replied as he disappeared up the stairs leaving a bewildered Mr Ellis staring after him.

'Where on earth did he learn to say "okey-dokey boss"?'

Tim turned bright red and hurried off to find something to do, leaving Mr Ellis to draw his own conclusions.

Upstairs, Siggy had reached Room Nine. He banged on the door and when there was no reply he marched straight in. Mr Johnson was still there, lying under the duvet, fast asleep. Sigurd bent over the unfortunate guest and shouted at him. 'Hey you! I clean beetroots. I clean today. You get up and go away!'

Mr Johnson stirred and groaned. 'What? What's going on? Look, I've got a stinking headache and I don't have to leave for another hour. Leave me alone. I'm going back to sleep.'

But the Viking wasn't having any of this. Mr Ellis had told him to collect the bed linen from Room Nine and that was exactly what he was going to do. Sigurd pulled out Nosepicker and pointed it at Mr Johnson. 'I clean beetroots!' he hissed.

'All right, go and clean beetroots if you have to, but leave me alone.' Mr Johnson sighed and turned over with a large groan.

Sigurd stared down at the poor guest. He pushed Nosepicker back into its scabbard and gritted his teeth. He reached down and grabbed all four corners of the bottom sheet. With one almighty heave he hoisted all the bedding, duvet and all, on to his shoulders, with Mr Johnson trapped inside and struggling to free himself.

'Hey! What's going on! Put me down you oaf!'

'I tidy!' shouted Siggy, stomping triumphantly downstairs.

'You're not tidy, you're filthy!' came a muffled voice from inside the duvet. 'Now let me out. Help!'

Mrs Ellis was the first to hear the cries coming from the back of the hotel and she hurried round to see what was going on. She was greeted by the sight of Sigurd striding into the laundry with a huge sack on his back. It was wriggling and shouting and had arms and legs popping out from all directions.

'Siggy? What is going on?'

The Viking grinned. 'I clean beetroot. This Room Nine.' So saying, he let the bundle fall to the floor.

'Ouch!' Mr Johnson struggled from the sheets, and after falling down three times because his feet were caught up, finally stood up in front of Siggy, red-faced and fuming. 'You idiot!' he yelled. 'You numbskull! Peabrain! Noodlebonce!'

Siggy stepped backwards as Mr Johnson marched towards him. 'I've never been in such an hotel!'

Mrs Ellis hastily tried to calm things down. 'I'm terribly sorry, Mr Johnson. Sigurd doesn't quite understand the rules of the hotel yet,' she said apologetically. 'Come with me and I shall make sure we give you a big discount on your bill.' As she took Mr Johnson gently by the arm and led him away she glared back at Sigurd. 'And you wait there and don't move!'

As soon as Mrs Ellis had finished with Mr Johnson she went off to find her husband. There was more serious talking to be done. 'I just can't cope with it all Keith. I am not going to spend the rest of my life giving our guests discounts because of that totally dopey Viking.'

Mr Ellis gave his wife a comforting hug. 'Don't worry. I think I've come up with a pretty good plan.' Penny Ellis glanced at her husband. 'You know how I've always complained about fetching and carrying guests to and from the station? Well, I thought I might teach Sigurd how to drive, and then he can do all that for us!'

'Are you sure Keith? I mean do you think Siggy could cope?'

'Of course, no problem! He'll love it. He'll take to it like a duck to water.'

'I just hope you're right,' murmured Mrs Ellis, already foreseeing disaster.

Siggy's first lesson was in the hotel carpark. Mr Ellis had taken the precaution of making sure there were no other cars parked there. Sigurd sat in the front seat looking terribly proud. He was quietly making 'brrrm brrrrm' noises into his beard and grinning madly at Mrs Tibblethwaite, who was standing by the back door watching.

'Think of it like a boat,' suggested Mr Ellis helpfully. 'This steering wheel controls the rudder.'

Sigurd appeared mystified. 'No oars. No sail. No boat. No float.' Mr Ellis wiped his forehead.

'No, well, perhaps not,' he said, beginning to wonder if teaching Sigurd to drive had been such a good idea after all. He took a deep breath. 'Listen, this wheel here makes the car go where you want it to. Understand?'

'Okey-dokey boss,' grinned Sigurd.

'Now, turn the key and start up the engine.' Mr Ellis pointed to the ignition switch. Sigurd gave the key a twist and the engine burst into life. So did Siggy. He shouted with delight and clapped his hands, bouncing up and down on the seat and going 'brrrm brrrrm' all over again. Mr Ellis tried to ignore him.

'This is the handbrake. Take it off like this. Put your foot on the clutch and push it down. That's right. Now we put the gear lever into first gear. See that other pedal? That's the accelerator pedal. Push it down gently and take your other foot off the clutch and weh-hey-whoa-ooohaaaargh. . . !'

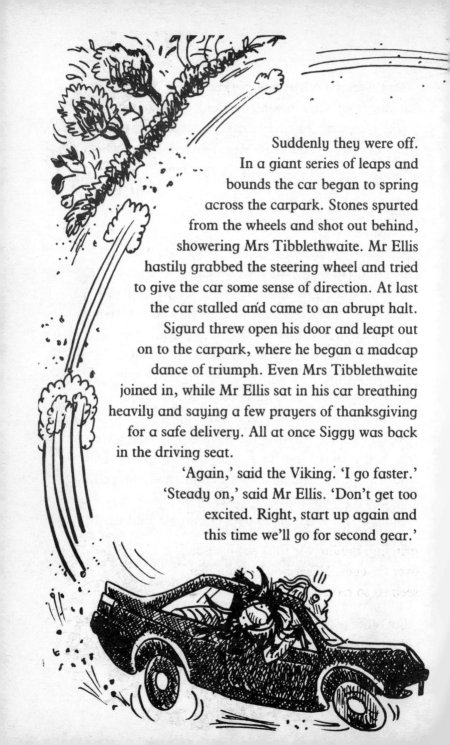

Suddenly they were off.
In a giant series of leaps and
bounds the car began to spring
across the carpark. Stones spurted
from the wheels and shot out behind,
showering Mrs Tibblethwaite. Mr Ellis
hastily grabbed the steering wheel and tried
to give the car some sense of direction. At last
the car stalled and came to an abrupt halt.

Sigurd threw open his door and leapt out
on to the carpark, where he began a madcap
dance of triumph. Even Mrs Tibblethwaite
joined in, while Mr Ellis sat in his car breathing
heavily and saying a few prayers of thanksgiving
for a safe delivery. All at once Siggy was back
in the driving seat.

'Again,' said the Viking. 'I go faster.'
'Steady on,' said Mr Ellis. 'Don't get too
excited. Right, start up again and
this time we'll go for second gear.'

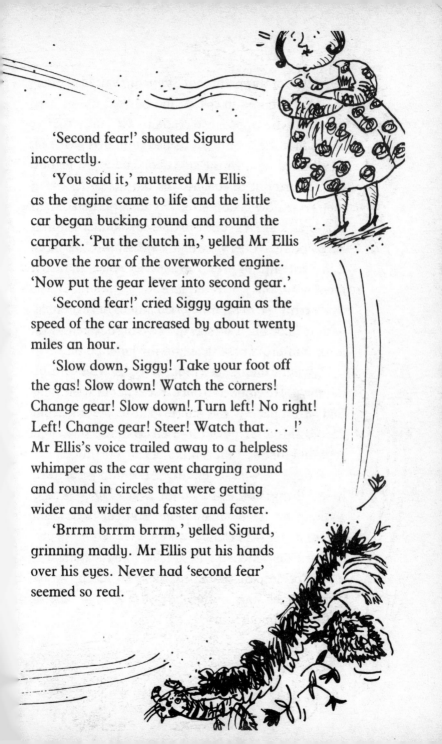

'Second fear!' shouted Sigurd
incorrectly.

'You said it,' muttered Mr Ellis
as the engine came to life and the little
car began bucking round and round the
carpark. 'Put the clutch in,' yelled Mr Ellis
above the roar of the overworked engine.
'Now put the gear lever into second gear.'

'Second fear!' cried Siggy again as the
speed of the car increased by about twenty
miles an hour.

'Slow down, Siggy! Take your foot off
the gas! Slow down! Watch the corners!
Change gear! Slow down!. Turn left! No right!
Left! Change gear! Steer! Watch that. . . !'
Mr Ellis's voice trailed away to a helpless
whimper as the car went charging round
and round in circles that were getting
wider and wider and faster and faster.

'Brrrm brrrm brrrm,' yelled Sigurd,
grinning madly. Mr Ellis put his hands
over his eyes. Never had 'second fear'
seemed so real.

It was at this point that Siggy grew tired of going round and round in circles and yanked the steering wheel in the opposite direction. The turn was so sharp that the car almost turned right over. Mr Ellis was hurled against the side door and when he next looked straight ahead he was alarmed to see that they were now heading for the hotel garden. There was a sickening crunch as the car bounced up the kerb and then they were on the grass. Mr Ellis made a last attempt to grab the steering wheel and save them both, but it was too late.

'Brrrm brrrm brrrrm!' cried Sigurd once more as, with a final burst of speed, the car shot across the lawn and did a nose dive into the hotel pond.

'Water!' announced Sigurd. 'Splish splash! I get out now.' He climbed from his seat out into the pond and struggled to the shore. The car sank a bit deeper. Mr Ellis pulled himself from the passenger seat and followed the Viking back to the hotel.

Sigurd looked back at the sinking car with great disappointment. 'That car no good,' he said, shaking his head. 'It no float. Bad car. I go clean beetroots for Mrs Ellis.'

Mr Ellis watched him squelch into the hotel with a look of despair. He knew that Mr Thripp would soon be back, but for now he didn't have the energy to do anything about it.

3

Deathsnore!

It took the breakdown truck over an hour to pull the car out of the hotel pond. Thankfully, apart from the car being rather wet not too much damage had been done. The car wouldn't start of course, and had to be towed to the garage to be dried out. Meanwhile, the Ellises were still left with the problem of how to employ Sigurd.

Tim suggested that maybe Sigurd could carry guests' bags up to their rooms, but Mrs Ellis was not so sure.

'I think that half the problem is that Siggy doesn't know how to talk to people normally. After all, he does come from the tenth century. It must be so difficult for him.'

Her husband gave a half-hearted smile and kissed his wife on the cheek. 'You're so forgiving. Sigurd does all these awful things and you forgive him.'

'That's because he's locked in a time-warp. You're not, Keith, and if you don't get that hedge trimmed soon YOU certainly won't be forgiven.'

'Ah – well I've had a really good idea about that hedge,' began Mr Ellis. 'I am going to hand over the gardening to Sigurd. It's ideal for him. A bit of grass cutting, some hedge trimming and so on – just the job.'

Mrs Ellis was doubtful. 'You may be right Keith, but knowing Sigurd you probably aren't. Give it a try anyway. He can't be any worse at it than he was at cleaning the bedrooms. Goodness me – look at Mrs Tibblethwaite, she doesn't look very happy. I wonder what's up.'

Mrs Tibblethwaite was indeed very unhappy and quite unlike her usual self. She hurried over to Mrs Ellis. 'I don't know what to do. I just don't know,' was all she could say.

'Please Mrs Tibblethwaite, do try and keep calm,' said Mr Ellis. 'Whatever's the matter?'

'I've just had this awful telephone call. I don't know what to do. My sister, you remember, she came to the wedding – she lives in Scotland. Well, her next door neighbour has just telephoned to say she's had a nasty fall. She's been taken to hospital with goodness knows what broken.' She turned her pale face towards Mr Ellis. 'What am I to do?'

Mr Ellis took her hands and squeezed them gently. 'You go and look after your sister, Mrs Tibblethwaite. She needs you. Go to the hospital and make sure she's all right. Take as long as you wish.'

Mrs Tibblethwaite nodded gratefully. 'But what about the. . . ?'

'The hotel will be fine,' added Mrs Ellis.

'I mean Sigurd,' whispered Mrs Tibblethwaite.

'What about my husband? He's such a child!'

'Leave him with us. He'll only be in the way if you take him to Scotland. He'll be fine with us,' said Mrs Ellis, secretly crossing her fingers behind her back as she spoke.

'Yes, we'll look after him,' said Tim. 'He can teach me sword fighting with Nosepicker.'

'Hmmm, very useful that will be!' muttered Mr Ellis.

'Oh thank you, thank you. I was hoping you'd offer to look after him,' said Mrs Tibblethwaite. 'I'll go and pack straight away and catch the first train from Flotby,' and with that she hurried upstairs.

Mrs Ellis watched her go.

'Siggy will be fine with us,' she repeated. 'Oh dear, why *did* I say that?'

Sigurd was almost uncontrollable when he realised that his dearest Tibby was going away for a few days. He tugged at his beard and wailed to the sky. 'Hear me Odin! Hear me Thor! Bring back Viking woman. I make you great sacrifice!'

'She's only going for a few days, Siggy,' Zoe pointed out. 'You're such a fusspot. You can help look after the hotel instead.'

Sigurd stopped. He straightened up and whipped out Nosepicker and thrust it into the air. Unfortunately it stuck in the ceiling but it was still a grand gesture. 'I am Sigurd the Viking,' he bellowed. 'I swear by all the gods that I will defend the hotel until the great day when Viking woman returns!'

It was a stirring speech, but quite meaningless, and when Sigurd yanked out Nosepicker from the ceiling and brought down half a ton of plaster, everyone wondered whether they really wanted him to defend the hotel anyway. Tim looked across at Zoe and rolled his eyes.

'He's a complete nutter,' he whispered to her.

'Takes one to know one,' Zoe replied as she disappeared out of the room in search of a bucket to put the plaster in. Meanwhile, Mr Ellis took Sigurd outside to show him the high hedge that ran round the edge of the garden.

'It needs a good trim, Siggy.'

'Good trim?' Siggy repeated, a little bewildered.

'Yes. Look, this is a hedge trimmer. It's electric.' Mr Ellis switched it on. Sigurd leapt back drawing Nosepicker and waving it violently at Mr Ellis as if he expected there to be a major battle. Mr Ellis laughed and switched the trimmer off. 'It's not going to attack you Siggy. Watch. This is how you use it.'

Mr Ellis switched the trimmer back on and began to slice neatly through the hedge. Twigs and leaves fell on every side. Sigurd watched closely. He thought this was marvellous. Mr Ellis put the machine into his hands and helped Sigurd guide the trimmer over the hedge.

'You see? It's easy with a hedge trimmer. Now, I want you to do the whole hedge, right the way round. Okay?'

'Okey-dokey boss.'

'I do wish you wouldn't say that,' said Mr Ellis as he turned to walk back to the hotel. But just as he was about to step inside, he heard the roar of the hedge trimmer and felt a sudden uneasiness. 'Do try and make a good job won't you, Siggy?' he said desperately.

'I make good job,' muttered Sigurd, as the hedge trimmer vibrated in his hands. Mr Ellis went into the hotel. He couldn't spend all day worrying about Sigurd – he had some plastering work to do.

For several moments Sigurd just stood there, marvelling at the wonderful machine that Mr Ellis had so carelessly placed in his raving Viking hands. A murderous glint came into Siggy's eyes and he looked wildly about the garden. The engine roared and Sigurd began to advance on the enemy.

Back in the hotel, the first person Mr Ellis saw was Mr Thripp. The thin little Health Inspector was back, complete with his tin-can voice. 'Good day, Mr Ellis,' he whined. 'I hope it's a good day for you?'

Mr Ellis managed a weak smile. 'Fine thank you, Mr Thripp. To what do we owe the pleasure of your company?'

'I have come about your "Viking". Not that he is a *real* Viking of course. I think it would be going too far to claim that.' Mr Thripp looked up sharply, his weasel eyes fixed on Mr Ellis.

'That's really no concern of yours,' replied Mr Ellis, trying to remain calm. 'Anyway, what can I do for you?'

'I have just come to make sure that this – "Viking" – is no longer a health hazard to your visitors, or I shall have to issue orders to close the hotel. I do hope he is no longer serving food?'

'Of course not. He's working in the garden,' replied Mr Ellis.

Mr Thripp gave a sneaky smile. 'You won't mind

if I check on that will you? It's not that I don't believe you. It's just that . . .'

'. . . you don't believe me,' finished Mr Ellis. 'Follow me, Mr Thripp, and you will see that Sigurd is quite harmless.'

The two men walked out into the garden. They stopped. They stood still. There was no garden. From the far corner could still be heard the murderous whine of the hedge trimmer as Sigurd sliced through the last few flowers, bushes, shrubs, hedges – in fact anything that was more than a few centimetres tall.

Mr Ellis could barely speak. 'What have you done?' he croaked. Sigurd gave a broad smile and switched off the hedge trimmer.

'I cut hedge like you show me! Zzzipp! Zzzapp! This better than Nosepicker. When Sigurd next go to war he take Deathsnore.'

'Deathsnore?' repeated Mr Ellis in a trance.

'I call new weapon Deathsnore. It make noise

27

like man snoring and bring death to everything – Deathsnore.'

Mr Ellis began to mutter to himself. 'I've got a mad Viking in my garden who has just destroyed every bush and flower with a hedge trimmer called Deathsnore. What am I going to do?' He was so overcome by the full-scale destruction of his garden that he didn't notice Sigurd's bulging eyes and purple face. The Viking had just seen Mr Thripp.

'You kill my weeding!' roared Sigurd. 'Now I kill you!' The hedge trimmer gnashed its teeth and Sigurd plunged after the Health Inspector. Mr Thripp gave a high scream and raced into the hotel, locking the door behind him.

'I kill you!' bellowed Sigurd. 'You very little man. I make you littler. I cut you into pieces like salami!'

It took Mr Ellis ten minutes to calm Sigurd and get Deathsnore away from him, and a further hour to calm Mr Thripp. The thin Health Inspector was shaking from head to foot.

'We shall see about this, Mr Ellis. I have never been threatened before and you needn't think that you will get away with it. He was going to chop me up with a hedge trimmer. I'm going straight to the police. That maniac should be in jail, and so should you. This hotel is a disgrace. It's not an hotel at all, it's a madhouse. You should all be locked up. I'm going to the police now. This isn't the last you've heard from Ernest Thripp. I shall be back, mark my words, and then there'll be trouble . . .'

The delirious inspector ran off down the hotel steps, shaking his fist and screaming at the top of his voice.

Mr Ellis slumped into an armchair and buried his face in his hands. 'If only this were just a bad dream,' he said to himself.

4

Sigurd Goes Berserk

Mr Thripp ran all the way to Flotby Police Station. 'Help, help! There's a Viking on the loose and he wants to chop me up like salami!' he screamed at the officer on the front desk.

Constable Pritty fixed Mr Thripp with a calm stare, 'I see, Sir. Would you like to take a deep breath and just tell me as calmly as you can what's happened?'

Mr Thripp glanced fearfully over one shoulder at the open door. 'I have just been to The Viking Hotel. There's a Viking there – at least there's a madman who says he's a real Viking and he tried to chop me up with Deathsnore.'

'Deathsnore? Excuse me sir, but what is Deathsnore?'

'A hedge trimmer.'

'A hedge trimmer?'

'Yes Officer, a hedge trimmer. For heaven's sake, open your ears and listen. You've got to do something about it.'

'This sounds very serious indeed, Sir. Attempted murder with a hedge trimmer. Can you describe the criminal?'

'Yes. He's revolting.' Mr Thripp said bluntly.

'Revolting,' repeated Constable Pritty. 'Do you think you could give me a few more details, Sir?'

'Yes. He's revolting, disgusting and filthy!' said Mr Thripp completely missing the point.

'No, no, Mr Thripp – can you describe what he looks like?' Quickly Mr Thripp described Sigurd more clearly. Constable Pritty was rapidly drawing on to a big sheet of paper as Mr Thripp spoke, and as soon as the Health Inspector had finished, Constable Pritty triumphantly held up his sketch.

'There! What about that? I don't think we shall have much trouble finding this lad. Of course it is quite impossible that he's a real Viking, so he's breaking the Trade Descriptions Act as well.'

Mr Thripp gave a sneaky smile. 'And he's a foreigner!'

'Foreign eh? We'd better check his passport then. He may be an illegal immigrant. Let's see, what have we got so far – attempted murder, contravening the Trades Description Act and being an illegal immigrant.' The constable licked the end of his pencil. 'Not to mention carrying an offensive weapon, namely one hedge trimmer,' he said, looking up triumphantly.

'I think your Viking chappie could be spending a long time in jail. Come on, let's go and arrest him.'

It was hardly a surprise to Mrs Ellis when she answered the knock on the hotel door to find Mr Thripp and a policeman standing there. The policeman pushed himself forward and adjusted his helmet. 'I'm Pritty, Madam,' he explained.

Mrs Ellis examined the policeman's young face carefully. 'Yes, I suppose you are pretty in a way – for a policeman that is.' The constable turned extremely red.

'That is not quite what I meant, Madam.'

'No, I don't suppose it was. Would you like to start again?'

'I am Police Constable Pritty and I am afraid that I have come about a very serious matter. I have come to arrest a Viking by the name of Sigurd.'

Mrs Ellis had never thought it would get quite as bad as this. She could tell from the sickening smile on Mr Thripp's face that there was big trouble in store for Sigurd, and she had no idea how to rescue him from this new situation.

'I'll fetch him for you,' she said quietly, and hurried off to find her husband.

Mr Ellis gritted his teeth at the news. 'Sigurd's in the garden planting some new bushes. I'll bring him to the hall.'

A few moments later Mr Ellis arrived with Siggy. His hands were covered in mud from the garden, where he had been digging. Mrs Ellis introduced everyone, hoping that Sigurd would make a good impression on the policeman. Siggy knew all about English good manners. He strode forward with a big grin on his innocent face and shook Constable Pritty warmly by the hand.

Unfortunately he left most of the hotel garden smeared across the constable's hand. The policeman gamely tried to wipe it off, only to put several large muddy streaks across the front of his uniform. 'Damaging a police officer's uniform – that's a very serious charge indeed,' muttered Constable Pritty, fumbling for his notebook.

Mr Ellis asked if there was a problem. Why did they need to arrest Sigurd? Constable Pritty immediately launched into a long description of all the charges, with Mr Thripp grinning and hopping excitedly from one foot to another and adding bits here and there. Finally Constable Pritty asked to see Sigurd's passport.

'Pass-the-pot?' repeated Siggy. Glancing round the hotel entrance he saw a rose bush standing in a big tub. Of course! That must be it! Sigurd seized the flowertub with both hands, picked it up and thrust it into Constable Pritty's chest. 'Pass-the-pot!' Siggy repeated excitedly, thinking this must be some new party game.

'What are you doing? Are you trying to be funny?' cried Constable Pritty. Sigurd nodded and grinned even more.

'I funny. You funny. Funny man in funny blue hat!'

Constable Pritty thrust out his chin and snapped at his helmet strap. 'I am not funny at all, and neither is my hat,' he growled.

Mr Ellis hastily came to Sigurd's aid. 'Sigurd doesn't have a passport, Officer. You see, it's not that he comes from another country, but that he comes from another century – the tenth century, and they didn't have passports then.'

'Oh yes? And my name is Darth Vader!'

'I thought he was taller,' murmured Mrs Ellis.

'This is not a laughing matter, Madam. This Viking will have to come down to the police station with me for questioning.'

Mr Ellis turned to Sigurd and tried to explain the situation to him, but Siggy would have none of it. 'I no go with Mr Blue-hat.'

'Insulting a police officer,' muttered Constable Pritty reaching for his notebook again. 'I'm afraid that you have no choice, Sir. Just come with me please and don't make things worse for yourself.'

It was at this point that Constable Pritty made a bad mistake. He tried to pull Sigurd along by the arm. In an instant Sigurd had leaped backwards, pulling Nosepicker from his scabbard as he did so.

'Hah!' yelled Sigurd. 'Death to my enemies and to the enemies of my enemies and the enemies of the enemies of enemies – I think. By Thor, I make you all into barbecue meat!'

It was no use trying to calm the Viking down now. His blood was up. He stood there waving Nosepicker over his head so violently that he cut down three hanging baskets. Constable Pritty and Mr Thripp stared in horror at the mad Viking warrior and slowly began to back down the path.

Constable Pritty was secretly delighted at all this. Flotby was such a boring town normally and now he had a full scale incident on his hands.

'I think reinforcements are called for,' he hissed to Mr Thripp. 'Come on, back to the station – fast!' The two turned tail and ran, leaving Sigurd standing on the hotel steps waving Nosepicker. Mr and Mrs Ellis looked desperately at each other.

By this time Tim and Zoe had come outside to see what all the fuss was about. When they heard that Sigurd was about to be arrested and taken away they were horrified.

'Do something, Daddy!' cried Tim.

'I can't. I don't know what to do,' wailed Mr Ellis.

'But he hasn't done anything wrong!' cried Zoe.

'No? What about chasing Mr Thripp with a hedge trimmer, not to mention trying to skewer a policeman with Nosepicker.'

'But that was self-defence,' argued Zoe.

'Smell the fence!' shouted Sigurd with a big grin.

'Not smell the fence – self-defence,' corrected Zoe. Sigurd nodded violently.

'Smell the fence!'

Mr Ellis buried his face in his hands. He could hear the wail of fast-approaching police cars. Tim stared out from the hotel steps. 'Quick!' he shouted. 'You've got to do a runner, Sigurd. They're after you.'

But Sigurd stood his ground. 'I no go. I no coward. If Blue-hat wants Sigurd he come and take him.' Sigurd slowly drew Nosepicker and strode to the front of the steps as six police cars burst on to the forecourt. Doors sprung open and twenty police officers leaped from the cars. Constable Pritty stood near the back with a megaphone.

'Give yourself up!' he shouted. 'There is no escape. You are outnumbered. It's twenty against one. Give yourself up!'

Sigurd's answer to this was quite extraordinary and took everyone by surprise. He started taking off all his clothes. He pulled off his boots. He pulled off his jacket. Then he removed his shirt and started on his leggings.

'What's he doing?' whispered Mrs Ellis.

'Taking all his clothes off,' said Mr Ellis, not quite believing what he was seeing. Zoe clutched at her father's arm.

'Daddy I know what he's doing! He's going berserk!'

'Berserk?' repeated Mr Ellis. 'He's stark raving bonkers if you ask me!'

'No, no! That's where the word berserk comes from. A "berserk" was a Viking warrior. When faced with terrible odds in a battle they took off all their clothes and then charged into the fight!'

'What an extraordinary thing to do, and what peculiar things you learn at school,' said Mr Ellis.

By this time Sigurd was sitting on the stone floor, pulling at his leggings and muttering to himself. 'I berserk warrior. I cover garden with blood of Mr Blue-hats!'

Seizing his chance, Constable Pritty shouted 'Charge!' and a line of twenty police officers pounded towards the steps of the hotel, while Sigurd desperately tried to make up his mind. Was he going to pull his leggings off, or pull them back on again?

5

Sigurd Makes His Escape

Yelling furiously because it made them all feel a lot braver, the policemen stormed the hotel steps. Sigurd struggled to his feet and pulled up his trousers. He waved Nosepicker violently. The police paused for a moment and watched the bare-chested Viking warily. Sigurd glared at each and every one with a murderous glint. Then suddenly he shouted 'Boo!', turned tail and vanished into the hotel.

'Charge!' squeaked Constable Pritty once more, and the police plunged after Sigurd, only to get completely jammed in the doorway. There was an awful lot of huffing and puffing and grunting and grumbling as they sorted out the pile-up. Then they were up and stumbling after the laughing Viking.

Sigurd was having a wonderful time. He raced up one staircase and reappeared at the top of a quite different set of stairs. He slid down the banisters, rushed through the kitchen, back into the hotel, up the stairs again, and in and out of the bedrooms causing astonished shouts from the guests. Then he went downstairs again, through the lounge, into the garden, up the fire escape . . . and all the time the number of people chasing him grew and grew, as guests came out of their rooms and joined in.

At last Sigurd decided he had done enough running. He cast a quick look over his shoulder to watch the long blue snake bobbing up and down on his trail, then he dipped along a short corridor and vanished, leaving nothing but a flapping door to show where he had passed.

Twenty policemen and fifteen guests ran panting into a small room only to find it completely empty. There was no sign of Sigurd apart from an open window. Constable Pritty rushed over and stared out into the garden. Siggy was standing down

there, waving to them all.

Constable Pritty gritted his teeth. There was no way he was going to leap down into the garden from this height. He rushed out to the stairs and raced down to the garden. Sigurd had vanished again. 'Search the place!' screeched the constable. 'He must be around here somewhere!' The policemen ran round and round the garden like escaped guinea-pigs, shaking their heads.

Mr and Mrs Ellis and Tim and Zoe knew exactly where Sigurd was and they couldn't bear to watch. Perhaps it was the terrible crashing of gears that finally gave the police the clue they so desperately needed.

A car engine whined furiously and, with a lot of wheel spin, one of the police cars suddenly rocketed from the hotel driveway. The siren blared and, with another ear-shattering scrunch of the gears, Sigurd whizzed out through the hotel entrance and on to the main road. Mrs Ellis covered her eyes. Tim and Zoe jumped up and down with excitement.

'Go on, Sigurd! Show them what you can do! Yeehah!'

The police watched in disbelief, until a frustrated cry from Constable Pritty sent them scurrying to the remaining cars. The air was filled with howling sirens, stones were catapulted from spinning wheels and five police cars set off in hot pursuit.

Slowly the sirens faded away and the dust settled on the hotel forecourt. Penny Ellis slipped one arm round her husband's waist. 'What happens now, Keith?' she asked. 'I don't think I can cope with much more.'

Mr Ellis stood staring out along the main road. At last he turned back to the hotel. 'I'm going inside. I'm going to make a pot of tea and I'm going to take three aspirins for my headache – that's what is going to happen next. Then we shall sit down and wait. I am quite certain that it will not be long before we hear from the police again.' Mr Ellis went wearily into the hotel. Zoe and Tim watched in silence as Mrs Ellis followed her husband. Tim looked up at his big sister.

'Trouble?' he asked.

'Big trouble,' said Zoe, and they sat down on the front steps and waited.

The car chase did not last long. Sigurd's driving had certainly not improved since he had taken Mr Ellis's car for a swimming lesson in the hotel duck pond. Before he had worked out how to steer he had driven straight down on to the beach. Startled holiday makers took to their heels, screaming in alarm, as the roaring, wailing police car bounced round and round and finally took off in a series of sand-churning zig-zags before plunging nose-first into the waves. Perhaps Sigurd thought this car might float and he could just carry on driving until he reached Denmark. Of course it didn't work. The car came to a full stop with an engine full of sea water. Sigurd opened the door, stepped straight into a large wave, fell over, choked, came up gasping and collapsed right into the arms of Constable Pritty, ably assisted by nineteen other officers.

Constable Pritty grinned. 'You're booked, my son!' There was a click of handcuffs and Sigurd was hauled away, bundled into a police car and whisked off to Flotby Police Station. The telephone call that The Viking Hotel was dreading came sooner than expected. Mr Ellis stood there with the telephone at one ear, grim-faced and looking very tired. It was Mr Thripp speaking from the other end, and he was obviously enjoying every moment of his triumph. At last Mr Ellis put the 'phone down. 'He's been locked in the cells. That's it. He doesn't stand a chance. The police don't take kindly to being threatened with swords and having their police cars stolen. What a mess! I don't know what to do now.' He slumped down in an armchair.

Mrs Ellis straightened up. 'I know what to do,' she said, going to the telephone. She dialled a long number which seemed to ring for ages before it was answered. 'Hallo?' said Mrs Ellis. 'Is that you, Mrs Tibblethwaite? It's Penny here. How is your sister?' There was a long speech from the other end, but at last Mrs Ellis said 'Oh good. I'm so glad she's making a good recovery. How is everything here? Well, we do have a little bit of a problem. Yes. Just a wee one. Sigurd is in prison . . .'

There was a yell of horror down the telephone that even Mr Ellis and the children could hear. On and on went the rantings and ravings. At length Mrs Ellis put the 'phone down and smiled across at her husband and children. 'Mrs Tibblethwaite is catching the next train to Flotby,' she announced.

'I don't see what good that will do,' said Mr Ellis gloomily.

'Well, put it this way, Keith. If you were Constable Pritty and you had just put Sigurd in a police cell, would *you* like to face Mrs Tibblethwaite and explain it to her?'

A slow smile spread across Mr Ellis's tired face. He kissed his wife on the cheek. 'You, Penny, are a clever and dangerous woman.'

'That's as maybe, but I'm not half as dangerous as Mrs Tibblethwaite when she's on the rampage!'

'Is there going to be a fight, Dad?' Tim asked. 'Can I join in? Is Mrs Tibblethwaite going to bash them all up?'

'Tim! That's not a nice way to talk at all!' interrupted Mrs Ellis. Tim sighed.

'I was only asking,' he grumbled.

'Well why don't you go and do something useful – like tidy your room – before we have to go and meet Tibby's train. Go on.'

Tim heaved another sigh and went upstairs. He tried tidying his room but he was far too excited. The next few hours of waiting were a nightmare.

But if Tim was bored with waiting at the hotel, it was nothing compared to the rage and frustration felt by Mrs Tibblethwaite as her train slowly made its way towards Flotby. She couldn't believe a train could move so slowly. When the ticket collector made his way down the carriage she even asked if he would like her to get out and push. He didn't think it was at all funny.

Mrs Tibblethwaite had spent the last few days nursing her sister, and already she felt that she had been stuck indoors for far too long, running backwards and forwards with cups of tea and hot-water bottles. She now had a great deal of unused energy, and as the train crawled into Flotby station the door was already open. Mrs Tibblethwaite leapt down on to the platform, suitcase in hand and galloped to the barrier where the Ellises were eagerly awaiting her arrival.

'Where is he? Where is my Siggy?' she cried.

Mr Ellis took her by the arm and steered her towards the car, which had only recently come back from the garage, not only working, but dry. As they all got in Mr Ellis told her the whole story.

Tibby sat in the back seat with tears struggling down her cheeks. She clenched and unclenched her fists, over and over again. Then she began to beat her knees with her fists and finally the back of the driver's seat. She nearly sent Mr Ellis through the front windscreen and the car over a red light.

'For goodness sake!' cried Mr Ellis. 'Be careful!'

'I'll kill that Mr Thripp! I knew it was all his fault. He's a mingy, mangy, mean little pipsqueak. I'll kill him!'

'That won't help much,' Mr Ellis pointed out. 'Listen. We'll go back to the hotel and have a nice cup of tea and sit down calmly and think it all through. What we need is a plan.'

6

The Bomb Falls

A cup of tea did little to calm Mrs Tibblethwaite. She sat at one of the dining tables drumming her fingers angrily on the polished surface. She hadn't even bothered to take off her coat. The Ellis's watched her, wondering what she was thinking, and what she was going to do.

Tim was the first to break the silence. 'Suppose we rush into the police station and shout "Fire! Fire!" Then everyone will come running out and we can nip in and rescue Siggy.'

'How do we unlock his cell?' Zoe demanded.

'We could saw through the bars.'

'Timmy! That's a crackpot idea.'

'Well you think of something better then – Brainybottom.'

Mrs Ellis threw a cold glance across the table at the children. 'Okay, that's enough, you two. We have enough problems without the two of you arguing.' Mrs Ellis turned to Tibby and patted her gently on the hand. 'Would you like another cup of tea?'

Mrs Tibblethwaite shook her head. It was plain to all that she was quietly seething inside, and they waited for her to explode. But she didn't. At last she pushed back her chair and picked up her handbag.

'I'm going down to the police station,' she announced. 'Mr Ellis, would you kindly give me a lift please?'

'What are you going to do?'

'I'm going to talk to them. I cannot believe that this policeman – Prettyboy, or whatever his name is – can be stupid enough not to realise what a terrible mistake has been made. I am quite sure it is all a simple misunderstanding. Come on. The sooner we go, the sooner this whole mess will be cleared up.'

There was no stopping Mrs Tibblethwaite now, so everybody piled into the car and Mr Ellis drove to the police station. Just as they expected Constable Pritty and Mr Thripp were both there. They were sitting behind the front desk eating some large cream cakes and looking very self-satisfied. Beyond the desk could be seen a row of cells. One of them had a very sad looking heap of smelly rags piled in the corner.

Mrs Tibblethwaite marched up to the desk and rapped on it with her knuckles. 'I believe you have my husband, Officer, and I would like him back if you don't mind.'

Constable Pritty was nonplussed. 'I'm very sorry, Madam. You must be mistaken. The only person we have here is . . . hmmm!' Constable Pritty glanced at Mr Thripp and they both began to snigger. 'I can only describe him to you as being a raving madman, dressed in the smelliest, filthiest, most ridiculous clothes you've ever seen. He thinks he's a Viking! What a laugh! We do see some nutters in here, Madam.'

Mrs Tibblethwaite smiled back at the grinning policeman. 'That nutter *is* my husband, Officer, and for your information he is not mad. He *is* a Viking. Kindly release him.'

Constable Pritty and Mr Thripp stared at each other. Mr Thripp had a chocolate eclair stuck halfway to his mouth. Both men looked across at the Ellis's.

'She's telling the truth,' said Mr Ellis helpfully.

'God's honour!' added Zoe.

'Cross our hearts and hope to die!' Tim put in for good measure.

Constable Pritty leaned forward across the desk, unwittingly putting his elbow right on a cream doughnut. Jam and cream splurted out on all sides. 'Well, Madam, I am afraid your husband is facing some very serious charges.' And he went through the whole list, finishing with, 'stealing a police car and trying to drown it'.

'But he didn't know he was doing anything wrong. He's a tenth century Viking!'

'Oh of course Madam! And I'm Donald Duck!'

Mrs Tibblethwaite was rapidly running out of patience. 'It was all done in self-defence,' she said wearily.

At that moment the ragged heap in the far cell burst into life and threw itself at the bars. 'Smell the fence!' bellowed Sigurd, shaking his bars as hard as he could manage.

'My poor Siggy!' cried Mrs Tibblethwaite, stretching her arms towards her imprisoned husband. 'What have they done to you?' She turned back to Constable Pritty and fixed him with a steely glare.

'Please let him out, Constable – I'm sure we can settle the whole thing in court. He is perfectly harmless. There's no need to keep my husband like some caged-animal.'

'Harmless!' squeaked Mr Thripp, having finally managed to swallow the chocolate eclair. 'He threatened me with a hedge trimmer!'

'Let him out!' snapped Mrs Tibblethwaite.

'No.'

Mrs Tibblethwaite plonked her heavy handbag on the desk. 'Do you know what this is, Officer?'

'It's a handbag, Madam,' replied Constable Pritty very coldly.

'Wrong. It's a blunt instrument . . .' hissed Mrs Tibblethwaite as she whirled it round her head like a Viking axe. 'And I use it for hitting stupid policemen over the head until they see some sense.'

She began to batter Constable Pritty so hard that he had to duck down behind his desk, where he hurriedly pushed the alarm button. A siren screeched through the building.

Sigurd rattled his bars in fury. 'Let me out! Don't you touch Viking woman! By Thor, I'll ring your telephone!'

Zoe shook her head. 'I think you mean that you'll wring his neck, Siggy.'

'Yes, yes! I ring neck and telephone! Leave Viking woman alone!'

Why Sigurd was making such a fuss was a mystery to the Ellis's because Constable Pritty and Mr Thripp were getting by far the worst of the battle as Mrs Tibblethwaite continued to batter them with her handbag.

But reinforcements were now arriving fast from other parts of the police station, and soon a major battle was under way.

Tim jumped up and down and shouted 'Fire! Fire!' just in case it helped, which it didn't. The rest of the family retreated to the safety of the far corner and waited for the inevitable to happen.

It was amazing how strong Mrs Tibblethwaite was, and Mr Ellis wondered where on earth she had learned all her wrestling tricks. Policemen went flying in every direction. She had the head of one gripped under one arm and was busy giving an armlock to another. But the odds were finally overwhelming.

It was sheer weight of policemen that won the day. They piled on top of Mrs Tibblethwaite until there was a huge seething blue mountain. Out came the handcuffs and a few moments later Tibby was pushed into the same cell as Sigurd. They clung to each other in a touching embrace.

Constable Pritty picked himself up from the floor, straightened his hat, and tried to appear calm and unmoved. Tim and Zoe managed to stop themselves from telling him that there was a rather squashed chocolate eclair sitting on his right shoulder like some weird giant caterpillar. 'Any more of you like to be put behind bars?' he asked.

Mr Ellis slowly shook his head. He went to the cell and peered through at Sigurd and Tibby. 'Don't worry. We'll have to leave you here for the time being until the matter comes up in court. We'll see you at the trial. I'm sure everything will be fine!' he said, trying to sound reassuring.

Mrs Tibblethwaite was surprisingly cheerful. 'That's all right Mr Ellis. You go and look after the hotel. I've got Siggy and he's got me, and that's all that matters!'

For the next few days The Viking Hotel was filled with a deep and gloomy silence. Even the guests wandered about with clouded faces. The main reason the hotel had so many customers was because of Sigurd. They liked to see the huge, hairy Viking wandering about the place getting into trouble and speaking his very strange version of English. Now that he was no longer there they realised how much they missed him. Even Mr Ellis felt it although he was the one who always had to deal with the problems Sigurd caused.

They missed Mrs Tibblethwaite, too. She was central to the smooth running of the hotel. In fact Mrs Ellis thought that if Tibby had not had to go and look after her sister all these problems would never have occurred.

Mr and Mrs Ellis found themselves rushing about working three times as hard as they used to. Tim and Zoe helped out as best they could but it was no fun for anyone. There was immense relief when at last the day of the trial came. Everyone from the hotel, even the guests, made sure that they had front row seats at the Flotby Courthouse for the trial of Sigurd and Mrs Tibblethwaite.

Mr and Mrs Ellis had to give evidence. They tried to tell the judge that Sigurd was a Viking from tenth century Hedeby. They tried to tell her the story of how Sigurd had come to The Viking Hotel in the first place.

The poor judge was obviously very confused, but it was Zoe who finally managed to convince her that the story was true. She spoke with simple honesty, about their life with Siggy over the last year and she told Judge Farley how she had taught Sigurd to speak and had learned about his home.

Judge Farley was very impressed and things seemed to be going well for Sigurd and Tibby. Then Constable Pritty and Mr Thripp took the stand and things went from bad to worse. Crime after crime was mentioned, the last one being 'causing a chocolate eclair to stick to a police officer's uniform'.

The Ellis's watched Judge Farley's face closely. It was getting sterner by the second. From time to time she glanced across at Sigurd and Mrs Tibblethwaite with a deep frown. She shook her head slowly and scribbled notes on her note-pad.

Mrs Ellis slipped her hand into her husband's and whispered to him. 'I don't like it, Keith. Look at the judge's face. I'm afraid Tibby and Sigurd are really for it this time.'

7

Here Come The Vikings!

'Sigurd of Hedeby,' began Judge Farley, 'you have been charged with several very serious offences. I have listened most carefully to all the evidence against you and it is quite clear that these crimes have taken place.'

Mrs Ellis gripped her husband's arm tightly. 'I told you – he's in for it now,' she whispered.

'Ssssh,' muttered Mr Ellis as Judge Farley continued.

'It is also clear to me that if I were a Viking warrior, hundreds of miles from home, in a strange country and, even worse, in a strange *century*, I might well have behaved in the same way, especially if I had come across Constable Pritty and Ernest Thripp.'

By this time the entire Ellis family were sitting on the edges of their seats, nervously grasping the hand rails in front. Judge Farley coughed and went on, while Constable Pritty and Mr Thripp slowly turned paler and paler.

'In the normal course of events the behaviour of these two men would have been quite correct. They both have jobs to do, and they were both doing them. But these events were *not* normal. They were faced with something that they simply could not understand. It was their own reactions that drove Sigurd, and Mrs Tibblethwaite to behave as they did. I therefore find both of the defendants NOT GUILTY.'

A huge cheer almost tore the courtroom apart. The hotel guests leapt up and down, laughing and kissing each other. Zoe, Tim and Mrs Ellis were all in tears and Mr Ellis sat silently shaking his head, unable to believe the verdict. The judge banged her hammer loudly to bring back some order.

'There still remains one problem which must be dealt with as soon as possible. Mr Thripp was quite correct to report Sigurd for handling food. The guests at The Viking Hotel may enjoy the novelty of being served by a Viking, but I am quite sure that they wouldn't enjoy a dose of food poisoning. It is most important to find Sigurd something harmless to do and I order that this must be done by the end of the week.'

So saying, Judge Farley rose and swept out of the courtroom, leaving Sigurd's supporters to carry on cheering and to dance their way out on to the streets of Flotby. A conga of excited guests swept up the High Street and back towards The Viking Hotel, while Sigurd and Mrs Tibblethwaite sat on the roof of the car and waved to the laughing crowds as they made their way home. Sigurd had actually asked if he could drive – Mr Ellis had flatly refused.

'Talk about nerve,' he muttered to himself.

Back at the hotel the party continued for a long time. Siggy was even allowed to drink champagne from a water jug. Zoe brought down some of her music tapes and soon the guests were dancing around the tables in the dining room. Siggy joined in, clomping around, and became so excited that he got Nosepicker out and seconds later it was firmly stuck in the ceiling – again. Siggy thought it was so funny he left it there.

'It's like King Arthur and the sword in the stone,' suggested Tim. Tibby threw her arms wide open and shouted across the room.

'Hear ye! Whoever pulls this mighty Nosepicker from the ceiling will be the future King of England!'

Everyone collapsed laughing, ate far too much food and dragged themselves off to bed exhausted.

The following morning there seemed to be an awful lot of headaches around. Mr and Mrs Ellis eyed each other gloomily across the breakfast table. 'I still don't know what we can find Sigurd to do,' complained Mrs Ellis. 'The judge said it had to be something harmless. That's impossible with Sigurd.'

Tim came marching into the room holding Nosepicker aloft. 'I am the future King of England!' he announced loudly.

'Ssssh,' murmured Mr Ellis. 'Can't you see we're suffering? Anyway, we are trying to think of something for Siggy to do.'

'Maybe Mrs Tibblethwaite can think of something,' said Zoe.

'After the way she battered those policemen the other day I'm beginning to wonder if she's as safe as she looks,' said Mr Ellis. 'The pair of them strike fear into the heart!'

Tim put down Nosepicker with a loud clunk. 'I've just had a thought,' he said.

'Stand-by everyone!' giggled Zoe. 'Tim's had an idea!'

'But it's a good one,' said Tim. 'I think Siggy and Mrs Tibblethwaite ought to become wrestlers.'

'Wrestlers?'

'Yes – wrestlers.'

'WRESTLERS?!'

'Like you see on television sometimes, a tag team. They can dress up like Viking warriors. They'd be brilliant.'

There was complete silence round the table. Zoe was about to burst out laughing when Mrs Tibblethwaite walked in. She was moving carefully and slowly, as if the soft pile of the carpet was unbearably painful to her feet. 'I feel as if there's a road drill inside my head,' she said. She sat down slowly. 'Why is everyone looking at me?' she asked.

'Tim thinks that you and Siggy ought to be tag team wrestlers,' said Zoe with a little laugh. Tim stuck his tongue out at her. Zoe smiled and stuck hers out too. Mrs Tibblethwaite held her throbbing head in her hands and looked across at Tim.

'Just at this moment I don't think I could wrestle a pillow and win. But when I am feeling better, Tim, you and I are going to sit down and have a long chat. I think you are a genius. It's the most exciting idea I have heard for ages. Now, if you don't mind, I shall go back to bed until the roadworks inside my head have finished.' Tibby got up and slowly left the room.

Mr and Mrs Ellis and Zoe stared across the table at Tim, who had a quite ridiculous grin across his entire face. 'I'm a genius,' he reminded them all, picking up Nosepicker once more. '*And* the future King of England!' Zoe snorted and stamped out of the room.

Days passed in a whirlwind of activity. Posters went up all over the town. They were in shop windows, on lampposts, on cars, everywhere. The lettering was bright yellow and black and there was a colour photograph of Sigurd and Mrs Tibblethwaite in full Viking wrestling gear.

In a large empty room at the hotel, Sigurd and Tibby practised hard. Their first match was coming up fast, and they were up against one of the country's top tag teams, Grabbit and Grind. The two Vikings worked very hard and by the time the day of the wrestling match arrived they felt they were ready for anything.

Flotby Hall was packed out. It seemed as if everyone in the town had come to see the local celebrity and his wife in their first wrestling bout. The Ellis family had front row seats, and were barely able to control their excitement. They were astonished to see that Constable Pritty, Mr Thripp and Judge Farley were all in the audience.

A great cheer swept through the crowd as the main lights went out and the spotlights came on. There was a fanfare of trumpets and Grabbit and Grind appeared. Then another huge cheer went up as Sigurd and Tibby marched down to the ring. 'Yeeeah!' squealed Tim, and the bell pinged for the first round, Sigurd up against Grabbit.

First of all they circled each other, then there was a thunderous bang as they crashed into each other. Their arms locked and their muscles bulged. They grunted and heaved and hurled each other round the ring.

Zoe covered her eyes with her hands and then hastily uncovered them because she couldn't see anything. The wrestlers changed over. Grind threw herself at Mrs Tibblethwaite and they both fell to the floor. 'Go on Tibby,' screamed Zoe, beating her fists on her legs. Mr Ellis leaned back a calm smile on his face. He slipped an arm round his wife's shoulders.

'Who'd have thought it would end like this?' he whispered to her. 'Look at those two in the ring. They are having the time of their lives. Tim was right and it was a brilliant idea. We've solved the hotel problem too. We shall have even more customers now thanks to Sigurd and Mrs Tibblethwaite. Even Constable Pritty and Mr Thripp seem to be enjoying themselves. It's wonderful.'

The bangs and thuds went on as Sigurd and Mrs Tibblethwaite battled away with their opponents. Sigurd was standing on the ropes, both arms raised to the ceiling. 'By the God Thor!' he yelled. 'I telephone your neck!' he bellowed at Grind.

'Telephone your neck?' repeated Mrs Ellis to Zoe.

'I think he means he wants to wring her neck,' Zoe explained.

Sigurd launched himself from the ropes and landed on top of Grabbit. 'Now I make sacrifice to Thor!' he cried.

'Oh dear,' groaned Mr Ellis. 'It looks as if Siggy can even turn a wrestling match into a disaster area. I can't bear to watch!' And Mr Ellis screwed up his eyes tightly and shoved his fingers in his ears, whilst all around him people cheered wildly as The Viking Warriors grappled their way to victory.

Siggy and Mrs Tibblethwaite stood proudly in the ring, arms above their heads in triumph. Everyone cheered and clapped until their hands were sore.

'Dad, Dad,' cried Zoe tugging at her father's arm. 'It's all right, you can open your eyes now. Siggy and Mrs Tibblethwaite have won – they're a success!'

'A success,' muttered Mr Ellis, staring at Siggy with a look of amazement.

'I suck eggs,' Siggy shouted to him, hugging Mrs Tibblethwaite and grinning madly.

Mr Ellis looked at his wife in despair. 'Do you think he'll ever be normal?' he asked.

'I shouldn't think so,' she said. 'Anyway, what does it matter, Siggy's a success just the way he is.'

Mr Ellis looked doubtful, but left Siggy to get on with things in his own peculiar way. For now, at least, it seemed the best way of coping with the daft Viking.

Choosing a brilliant book
can be a tricky business...
but not any more

www.puffin.co.uk

The best selection of books at your fingertips

So get clicking!

Searching the site is easy – you'll find
what you're looking for at the click of a mouse,
from great authors to brilliant books and more!

Everyone's got different taste . . .

I like stories that make me laugh

Animal stories are definitely my favourite

I'd say fantasy is the best

I like a bit of romance

It's got to be adventure for me

I really love poetry

I like a good mystery

Whatever you're into, we've got it covered . . .

www.puffin.co.uk

hotnews@puffin

Hot off the press!
You'll find all the latest exclusive Puffin news here

Where's it happening?
Check out our author tours and events programme

Best-sellers
What's hot and what's not? Find out in our charts

E-mail updates
Sign up to receive all the latest news
straight to your e-mail box

Links to the coolest sites
Get connected to all the best author web sites

Book of the Month
Check out our recommended reads

www.puffin.co.uk

Read more in Puffin

For complete information about books available from Puffin – and Penguin – and how to order them, contact us at the appropriate address below. Please note that for copyright reasons the selection of books varies from country to country.

www.puffin.co.uk

In the United Kingdom: Please write to Dept EP, Penguin Books Ltd,
Bath Road, Harmondsworth, West Drayton, Middlesex UB7 ODA

In the United States: Please write to Penguin Putnam Inc., P.O. Box 12289,
Dept B, Newark, New Jersey 07101–5289 or call 1–800–788–6262

In Canada: Please write to Penguin Books Canada Ltd,
10 Alcorn Avenue, Suite 300, Toronto, Ontario M4V 3B2

In Australia: Please write to Penguin Books Australia Ltd,
P.O. Box 257, Ringwood, Victoria 3134

In New Zealand: Please write to Penguin Books (NZ) Ltd,
Private Bag 102902, North Shore Mail Centre, Auckland 10

In India: Please write to Penguin Books India Pvt Ltd,
11 Panscheel Shopping Centre, Panscheel Park, New Delhi 110 017

In the Netherlands: Please write to Penguin Books Netherlands bv,
Postbus 3507, NL–1001 AH Amsterdam

In Germany: Please write to Penguin Books Deutschland GmbH,
Metzlerstrasse 26, 60594 Frankfurt am Main

In Spain: Please write to Penguin Books S. A., Bravo Murillo 19,
1° B, 28015 Madrid

In Italy: Please write to Penguin Italia s.r.l.,
Via Felice Casati 20, I–20124 Milano

In France: Please write to Penguin France S. A.,
17 rue Lejeune, F–31000 Toulouse

In Japan: Please write to Penguin Books Japan, Ishikiribashi Building,
2–5–4, Suido, Bunkyo-ku, Tokyo 112

In South Africa: Please write to Longman Penguin Southern Africa (Pty) Ltd,
Private Bag X08, Bertsham 2013